DO THE WHALES STILL SING?

Dianne Hofmeyr ◆ PICTURES BY Jude Daly

Dial Books for Young Readers New York

Published by Dial Books for Young Readers
A Division of Penguin Books USA Inc.
375 Hudson Street
New York, New York 10014

By arrangement with The Inkman,
Cape Town, South Africa

Designed by Ann Finnell
Printed in Hong Kong
First Edition
1 3 5 7 9 10 8 6 4 2

Library of Congress Cataloging in Publication Data
Hofmeyr, Dianne.
Do the whales still sing? / by Dianne Hofmeyr ; pictures by Jude Daly. — 1st ed.
p.   cm.
Summary: An old man tells the lighthouse boy about a successful
sea captain who made his fortune hunting whales.
ISBN 0-8037-1740-7 (trade).—ISBN 0-8037-1741-5 (library)
[1. Whaling—Fiction. 2. Whales—Fiction.]
I. Daly, Jude, ill.   II. Title.
PZ7.H6797Do   1995   [E]—dc20   94-4576   CIP   AC

The full-color artwork was prepared using gouache.
It was then scanner-separated and reproduced
as red, blue, yellow, and black halftones.

For Michael
D. H.

For my father, Captain Robert Kenny
J. D.

On days when the wind blew wild and the sea swept past the point, Pete, the lighthouse boy, searched the sand for bits and pieces washed ashore by the waves. He collected strange sea-encrusted shells and gathered driftwood for an old man who sat carving each day against the hull of a time-worn boat.

"Have you always made things?" Pete asked one afternoon as he watched the man's strong, cracked hands at work on a piece of drift-wood.

Instead of answering, the old man kept carving, and told this story....

There was once a fierce and fearless sea captain who had harpooned more whales than he could ever remember.

Whenever a whale was sighted, the captain swiveled the harpoon gun, took aim, and fired. In his hands the harpoon was always on target.

When the whale leaped forward, heaving and pulling at the rope, his strong hands battled to reel it in. When the whale was too tired to fight any longer, he tied the body alongside the boat and dragged it back to shore.

At the factory, oil was made from the whale's thick blubber and sold for a high price.

Every time the rugged captain harpooned another whale, he scratched a small outline of one into the wood of his ship. Eventually there were too many whale scratchings to count, and he was a very rich man.

By day the captain was a fierce hunter, but by night out on deck under the stars he was a music-maker. His strong hands skillfully shaped music that flowed from his wooden flute.

Sounds of the stormy ocean filtered through his fingers, of sailors singing, of sails shuddering in the wind, of the harpoon rope hissing. It was the song of a whaler.

Then one quiet starlit evening as he stood playing his flute, a strange thing happened. He heard mysterious sounds coming up from the water all around his boat. They thrummed the dark depths and trilled the winds. They whispered the waves and serenaded the stars.

Together, sea music and flute music floated up into the air, louder and louder, reaching out into the night. The captain paused in his playing. His hands rested lightly around his flute.

Three whales broke the still surface of the water. The moonlight glistened over their bodies as they sang their mystical song.
The captain bent his head to catch the magical sounds.

He had heard such music a long time ago when he was a boy. He remembered the sweet sounds of his mother's lullaby and the melody of his father's voice.

Dawn came and still the whales sang. But the captain did not reach for his harpoon gun. He had heard their song. It had entered his heart forever. Instead he took up his flute and found pleasure in sounds that trilled the winds and serenaded the stars. Gone was his hunger for hunting. Gone was his desire for killing. It was time to find another way to live, and he felt at peace.

"Did he ever harpoon another whale?" asked Pete. The old man shook his head. Suddenly the boy noticed the pattern of countless whales behind the man along the edge of the hull. Pete looked back into the old man's face. "And do the whales still sing for him?"

The old man held out the carving that had taken shape in his cracked hands.

He smiled gently and replied, "Yes. They still sing for him."